W9-AWR-360

KIDS CAN'T STOP READING
THE CHOOSE YOUR
OWN ADVENTURE® STORIES!

"Choose Your Own Adventure is the best thing that has come along since books themselves."
—Alysha Beyer, age 11

"I didn't read much before, but now I read my Choose Your Own Adventure books almost every night."
—Chris Brogan, age 13

"I love the control I have over what happens next."
—Kosta Efstathiou, age 17

"Choose Your Own Adventure books are so much fun to read and collect—I want them all!"
—Brendan Davin, age 11

And teachers like this series, too:
"We have read and reread, worn thin, loved, loaned, bought for others, and donated to school libraries our Choose Your Own Adventure books."

CHOOSE YOUR OWN ADVENTURE®
AND MAKE READING MORE FUN!

Bantam Books in the Choose Your Own Adventure® Series
Ask your bookseller for the books you have missed.

Bantam Books in the Choose Your Own Adventure® Super Adventure Series

LONGHORN TERRITORY

BY MARC NEWMAN

ILLUSTRATED BY FRANK BOLLE

A BANTAM BOOK®

TORONTO • NEW YORK • LONDON • SYDNEY • AUCKLAND

RL 4, IL age 10 and up

LONGHORN TERRITORY
A Bantam Book / November 1987

*CHOOSE YOUR OWN ADVENTURE® is a registered
trademark of Bantam Books, Inc. Registered in U.S. Patent and
Trademark Office and elsewhere.*

*Original conception of Edward Packard.
Cover illustrations by George Wilson.
Interior illustrations by Frank Bolle.*

ISBN 0-553-26904-6

Published simultaneously in the United States and Canada

---

*Bantam Books are published by Bantam Books, Inc. Its trade-
mark, consisting of the words "Bantam Books" and the por-
trayal of a rooster, is Registered in U.S. Patent and Trademark
Office and in other countries. Marca Registrada. Bantam
Books, Inc., 666 Fifth Avenue, New York, New York 10103.*

PRINTED IN THE UNITED STATES OF AMERICA

O   0 9 8 7 6 5 4 3 2 1

For my mother

WARNING!!!

Do not read this book straight through from beginning to end! These pages contain many different adventures you may have when you spend the summer with your uncle Matt in a western town called San Talpa.

As you read along you will be able to make choices, and the adventures you have will be the result of those choices. Beware! The West in the year 1860 is a dangerous, unsettled place, and you'd better remember that before deciding whether to become deputy to the sheriff or a daring rider on the Pony Express!

Good luck!

You are in a stagecoach rattling along the dusty lains of the Old West. It's the year 1860. School t out two weeks ago, and you've spent the time aveling from your home in the East. You're going o spend the summer with your uncle Matt in the estern town of San Talpa. He's the sheriff, so our stay should be exciting!

The long journey is almost over, you think as an Talpa pops into view. Five minutes later the age shudders to a stop in the middle of town.

You spot your uncle Matt right away by the eaming silver badge on his chest. Matt is tall and black handlebar mustache frames his upper lip. lis tanned face tells you that he spends a lot of me in the sun.

"Uncle Matt!" you cry as you step out of the age.

Your uncle's eyes light up in recognition. He rings forward to give you a firm handshake. hen Matt leads you to where you'll be living for e next few months: the San Talpa jail!

Turn to page 2.

2

The jail is a small one-story building on the edge of town. A sign in the window says DEPUTY WANTED. Inside you notice a rifle rack where several Winchester carbines are stored. Three small unoccupied cells line the back wall. They look very clean. The keys to the cells are hanging on the wall.

After you drop your bags Matt says, "You must be starved! Let's get something to eat at Caroline's café."

Turn to page 6

It's over in a second. Jed blows the smoke from his pistol, picks up Coltrain's limp body, and walks out. He mounts up, tips his hat to you, and rides off.

You gather your horse and belongings and start for San Talpa. Now you have an exciting story to tell!

The End

4

"I'll stay and watch the town," you say.

"I'll be back in three days," Uncle Matt tells you that night.

When you get up in the morning, Matt is gone. You fix yourself a big breakfast of ham and eggs and sit down to eat.

Just as you finish putting away the dishes a rider rushes up to the jail, hastily ties up his horse, and rushes through the door.

"Deputy!" he cries. "The Burrows Gang was seen heading this way!"

The Burrows Gang! With alarm you remember what Matt told you about them; he said the gang was a band of hardened criminals who robbed stagecoaches. You realize that the nine o'clock stage from Wheelerville is a likely target of the Burrows Gang! You'd better meet the stage and escort it safely into San Talpa.

"The sheriff has gone to visit the outlying ranches," you tell the rider as you grab your gun belt and buckle it on. "Fetch him at once!"

Turn to page 10.

A few minutes later you and Matt seat yourselves at a small table in the café.

Matt calls hello to the owner, Caroline Pierce.

"Why, hello Matt," she replies cheerfully, then turns to you. "This must be the relative I've heard so much about. Welcome to San Talpa! Say, Matt, have you found a new deputy yet?"

"No," Matt answers. "I haven't been able to replace Pete Walters since he took the sheriff's post at Jacksonville."

"I could be your new deputy for the summer," you say.

"Are you serious?" Matt asks.

You tell him that you are.

All he says is "We'll see."

Turn to page 108.

You choose to wait until night, gambling that you are not scheduled to be executed until tomorrow. Just as night falls you sense that an Indian is right behind you.

"Don't move! I'm cutting you loose," he warns. "I'm setting you free."

"Why?" you ask.

"This fighting is wrong. Neither side is right. We need to negotiate an end to our differences. I'm trusting you to take this message to the commander of Fort Carson."

Gratefully you whisper thanks and slip away. Five minutes later you are on a stolen horse pounding toward Fort Carson.

Turn to page 97.

"Put your hands up!" you shout with your badge in one hand and your pistol in the other.

You find out that the Burrows Gang has no respect for the law as they start to level their guns at you. You manage to drill one before you are gunned down.

You had no chance.

The End

The rider hurries to do what you say. In a minute you're out of town, riding hard for the stage. As the wind blows through your hair you have a decision to make. If you cut across Indian Gulch, you could intercept the stage there and save time—providing the stage hasn't already reached the gulch. But if the stage is making good time, you could meet it at a location closer to San Talpa.

If you decide to cut across Indian Gulch, turn to page 74.

If you decide to meet the stage six miles from San Talpa, turn to page 81.

In the morning the sounds of frantic activity wake you. The owner of the ranch, Jack Miller, is shouting, "Rustlers stole twenty of my prize longhorns last night! You've got to do something, Sheriff!"

"Have some of your men saddle up," Matt barks. "I'll need their help."

Then Matt turns to you. "Well, Deputy, one of us must try to track the stolen steers. The other should ask around at the surrounding ranches to see if anyone saw anything. Which job do you want?"

If you decide to track the rustled cattle, turn to page 36.

If you decide to check the nearby ranches, turn to page 41.

You accept Matt's offer of training. Now you have to prove to your uncle that you can handle the job. For two weeks you practice his craft. You spend hours riding a horse and shooting all kinds of guns. He gives you dozens of practical tips on everything from desert survival to tracking. At night you pore over lawbooks, trying to learn everything you can.

Finally the moment of decision comes. Matt looks at you. A grin breaks out across his face.

"You will be a good deputy," he says.

It's the happiest day of your life. Matt gives you what you will need to uphold your duties as deputy: a repeating rifle, a pistol, and a horse. He also hands you a deputy's badge and solemnly swears you in as a lawman.

"You have the duty to protect all the citizens in the area. Always be courteous and fair. It's now your job to enforce the law. Good luck!"

Turn to page 19.

"I will," you say bravely. You take Jed's gun and walk in.

Inside the saloon you spot Coltrain right away, even though he has changed into a red shirt and blue jeans. His back is to you because he is drinking at the bar. Your gun hangs at his side.

You walk over to him, draw the bounty hunter's gun, and press the barrel against Coltrain's head.

"Coltrain, you're under arrest for breaking jail and stealing my horse!" you say.

Coltrain offers no resistance. In fact, he seems stunned that you—the one he left helpless in the mountains—are arresting him.

The End

Matt nods after you tell him your decision. "Good choice, Deputy. I figure the gang is hiding somewhere in the mountains. If we head out now, we'll have plenty of time to search before sundown."

You and Matt ride to the nearby mountains in silence.

"We can cover more territory if we split up," your uncle says. "If you find the gang, don't do anything foolish. We'll need a posse to deal with them. We'll meet back here at sunset."

Turn to page 20.

16

Pain, pain, pain. Those are the first three things you feel as you regain consciousness. Your hands are tightly tied to a pole that is driven into the ground. Your head is throbbing and your vision is blurred.

Two Indians are pointing excitedly at you and jabbering in their own language. Another Indian walks over and makes menacing gestures with his hunting knife. You have a feeling that you've been spared—only to be tortured sometime soon!

Turn to page 24.

18

You don't trust Henry Parker one bit. He seem to be hiding something, and his North Pasture seems to be a good place to start looking. You decide to sneak over there while the men from the DL Ranch wait.

You are at the edge of the North Pasture when you hear three riders coming up from behind you. It's Henry Parker and two of his men.

"What are you doing over here?" Henry demands. "I told you to stay away from the North Pasture."

"I just want a look around," you state boldly.

"All right, I'll show you around," Henry says.

Turn to page 96

Two weeks and four days have passed since Matt decided you were ready to wear a deputy's badge. Since then you've done all the small duties that come with the job, like patrolling the town and cleaning the jail, but nothing has disturbed the peace. You are getting bored.

After lunch Matt says, "I'm going to check on some of the outlying ranches tomorrow. Do you want to come? It's just a routine check, but it would give you a chance to see more of the West. If you'd rather, you can stay in town instead and mind the fort."

If you decide that it would be fun to go with Matt, turn to page 37.

If you'd like some independence for a change, turn to page 4.

20

Matt heads west, and you begin your eastbound search up a towering peak. The midday sun feels warm on your neck and shoulders as your horse climbs the mountain.

Late in the day you come upon an abandoned mine shaft. It doesn't look as if the gang is hiding out here, but your training as a deputy has taught you not to overlook any possibility. Should you stop to investigate it? you wonder. If you do, you won't have time to cover the whole mountain before sundown.

If you search the mine, turn to page 40.

If you decide to continue up the mountain, turn to page 89.

In the morning you head toward San Talpa's Pony Express office. As you push open the door of the weather-beaten building, a bell rings over your head. The walls of the place are bare, except for a few paintings of western scenes: Indians, covered wagons, antelope, buffalo, and so forth.

A big man is working at a desk in a corner of the room. At the sound of the bell he looks up and asks, "Can I help you? I'm Mr. Tucker."

"Yes," you reply. "Your sign in the window says that you need a rider. I'd like that job."

"Are you sure? Riding for the Pony Express can be very dangerous. Just last week a rider was killed during a robbery."

You summon all your courage and say, "Yes, I'm sure. When can I start?"

"You can start in the morning. Right now, I'll tell you all about your new job."

Turn to page 109.

You must escape. When the Indians aren't looking, you break off one of your spurs against the ground. Then you slide down the pole and pick the spur up off the ground. Straightening up, you slowly begin to cut your ropes. About an hour before sundown you have only a few strands to go. You won't cut them until you make your escape attempt.

After your ropes are completely cut, you can make a break for a horse right away and try to get to Fort Carson. Or you could break for the hills on foot and hide out. You'd probably be able to escape, but you'd never make it to the fort. If you wait until night, it would be easier to escape, but the Indians may have different plans for you before nightfall!

If you dash for a horse, turn to page 105.

If you head for the hills, turn to page 93.

If you wait until night, turn to page 7.

You turn your horse around and speed off.

Within half an hour you find your way blocked by a temporary Indian camp. Hundreds of Indian warriors are assembled. The sheer size of this force is frightening.

Now you have to decide between spying on the Indians in order to estimate their numbers or continuing on to Fort Carson. The Indian camp is directly ahead of you, so if you continue on, you'll also have to choose your direction.

If you stay and spy, turn to page 84.

If you head to Fort Carson and skirt the camp on the right, turn to page 104.

If you head to Fort Carson and skirt the camp on the left, turn to page 63.

It's been a peaceful vacation these past three weeks now that the Burrows Gang is out of your hair. You often go swimming in the mountains where a stream forms a pool of water. Every other day you write a letter back home telling your family about this, your best summer vacation ever.

Every day you practice the skills of a lawman. You study the lawbooks every night. During the day you practice riding and marksmanship.

You can now stand on the back of a moving horse. You can also use a lasso well from horseback. Riding without a saddle, or bareback, is easy for you.

You can almost outdraw Matt now, and when you throw a silver dollar in the air, you can hit it more often than not.

The rest of your time is spent in the Bucking Bronco Saloon drinking sarsaparilla.

Turn to page 35.

Sullenly you head back to the ranch house. When you arrive, you are surprised to see Matt and about ten ranchers smiling at you. The foreman is quickly disarmed.

"Mr. Parker is in the next room," Matt says. "He's under arrest for cattle rustling. The trail led here," Matt explains. "It was easy to round up the criminals after that."

The End

"Ride for it!" you scream to the driver. You unsling your rifle and unleash a barrage of bullets on the highwaymen. One of the robbers is hit and topples from his horse. Another of the robbers goes to his aid, but the two remaining men return your fire.

The two remaining desperadoes are closing, so you turn your horse around and make for the rapidly disappearing stage. It's going to be a tight race to San Talpa—you have less than two miles to go, and the lead, but their horses are much more rested than yours.

You catch the stage with a mile to go. The man riding shotgun is now lying prone on top of the stage, steadying his rifle. Once he opens fire, the crooks drop back out of his range.

As soon as San Talpa comes into view they give up the chase.

Turn to page 59.

"Not much farther to go," one cowboy says to the prisoner.

The rest of the cowboys laugh.

"What's going on here?" you ask forcefully.

"We've caught us a horse thief red-handed. We're going to string him up!" a cowboy tells you.

You remember what Matt told you about vigilantes:

"Vigilantes take the law into their own hands and act as judge, jury, and executioner. That is wrong. Sometimes vigilantes kill innocent people. Sometimes the punishment they give is too severe for the crime. The only true justice is decided in a courtroom according to the law, not by a mob with a rope."

"That man is going to stand trial in San Talpa, not swing from that tree," you state.

"No! This jasper's going to pay—right here!" one shouts.

The others roar their approval.

"Stay out of our way!" one warns you.

What will you do now? It would be very dangerous to try to stop this inflamed vigilante mob. Yet how can you let this man die? You were taught that people are innocent until proven guilty.

If you try to save the man, turn to page 34.

If you stand by and say no more, turn to page 101.

You draw your gun and set off down the right-hand passage.

"Arrgh!" you cry as you trip over something and land hard on your arm. You feel the wooden handle of the discarded miner's pick you tripped over. Holding your aching arm, you sit still and listen to see if anyone heard your cry of pain.

The mine is silent for a full minute. Then you hear muffled voices from outside the mine. It may be the Burrows Gang returning to their hideout! With renewed purpose you head down the tunnel to hide.

Turn to page 49.

Hours later you trudge into the trading post. The owner quickly gets you a glass of water.

After you've downed the water, the owner asks you about your horse.

"It was stolen," you answer shamefaced. "I was hoping to get a ride back to San Talpa."

"The thief—he wouldn't happen to have been wearing gray, now, would he?" another voice adds.

You look up into a pair of steely eyes. A man towers over you. He wears his gun low on his hip, and he has a look of confidence and determination about him. His face is unshaven and heavily weathered.

"Yes, he was dressed entirely in gray," you answer.

"C'mon then, let's get your horse back," the man says.

He walks outside and mounts a light reddish-brown horse, a sorrel. Then you climb on behind him.

You direct the man to the spot where your horse was taken. He examines the mud near the stream and locates your horse's trail. Soon you are in hot pursuit! Each second takes you farther from San Talpa, but you don't care—you want your horse back!

Turn to page 57.

34

"No! Vigilantism is wrong!" you say firmly as you draw your pistol. "I'm the deputy of San Talpa, and I'm taking him in." You pause to let your words take effect. "If any man tries to stop me, I'll have him arrested for obstructing justice. Now, who's going back to San Talpa to press charges against this man?" you ask, pointing to the prisoner.

All the men mutter excuses and quickly disperse. Obviously no one actually saw him steal a horse.

You get the frightened man some water and give him a ride back to San Talpa. He tells you his name is Joe Wilson, and he's been looking for work the past few weeks. He has no family.

You arrange for Joe to spend the night at the Silver Dollar Hotel. The next morning he tells you that he's decided to settle in San Talpa. Caroline Pierce has already given him a job as a cook at her café.

Turn to page 65.

Lately you've been spending your afternoons exploring outside of town.

"Well," Matt says during lunch, "where are you headed today?"

"North of town," you respond. "I may go all the way to Fort Carson."

"You shouldn't have any problem reaching the fort and getting back here by nightfall if you leave soon," Matt says. "I've never seen anyone take to riding as fast as you have."

You leave soon after lunch with your canteen full and your guns loaded.

Turn to page 64.

The rocky ground makes it nearly impossible for you to follow the cattle's trail—even with the help of some of the cowboys. After a full day of tracking you determine that the stolen cattle crossed onto cattle rancher Henry Parker's land. He is one of the richest ranchers around.

You decide to question Mr. Parker, a short, heavyset man with dark features. When you ask him about the stolen cattle, he becomes furious. Shouting angrily, he says, "I don't know a darn thing about your rustled cattle! And my men don't either!"

Deciding that the rancher isn't about to give you any information, you curtly thank him for his time and begin to turn your horse around.

"Wait," Mr. Parker calls, suddenly sounding more friendly. "Try searching south tomorrow. But stay out of my North Pasture. My men are mending fences out there."

Turn to page 75.

Early the next morning you and Matt ride leisurely out of town toward the nearest ranch.

At the edge of the DL Ranch, you encounter a band of cowboys branding cattle.

"Hey, Matt," a tall cowboy yells. "Who's that with you?"

"This is my new deputy. The kid's a real hard worker and good with a gun," Matt responds.

Turn to page 51.

The rancher begins to gallop forward, and you follow, letting him slip away. When he has a fifty yard lead, you wheel around and head back to the herd.

You are not surprised to find the DL brand on the steers' flanks.

Henry and his two men are hurrying toward his ranch house. They know the jig is up and are trying to escape before you can get help.

You are in luck because you find six of your men in the next field. With their help you round up Henry and his entire gang of rustlers. Jack Miller is ecstatic over the recovery of his prize longhorns.

"Name your reward," he says to you.

"No reward is necessary. It's my job to protect the honest citizens of this territory," you answer.

The End

You decide that you can't overlook any possibility, so you hide your horse a short distance from the entrance of the mine and cautiously head into its black mouth.

You proceed carefully, groping along, because only a small amount of light filters in. Up ahead you notice that the tunnel splits into two shafts.

You stop at the fork and listen. You think you hear faint moaning coming from the left-hand passage, but you're not sure. You hear nothing from the right-hand tunnel, but you do feel a slight breeze from that direction.

Which tunnel should you investigate first?

If you choose the right tunnel, turn to page 31.

If you choose the left tunnel, turn to page 78.

You decide to check out the neighboring ranches. You don't find anything suspicious at the first two ranches you check. The next ranch is owned by Henry Parker, one of the most powerful men in the area.

"No. There aren't any rustlers around here, youngster," he claims. "Now, get off my land. I'm a busy man."

Mr. Parker seems very eager to be rid of you. You wonder if he's hiding something. You could question his men to see if they know anything about the missing cattle, or you could secretly investigate Mr. Parker's land.

If you look around, turn to page 70.

If you question the men, turn to page 66.

The next morning you and Matt meet the stage at Wheelerville. You quickly explain your plan to the driver. He hastily agrees and you climb aboard. You are going to be an extra guard on the stage, along with the man riding shotgun next to the driver. Matt is going to follow the stage on his horse. If the Burrows Gang is about to stick the stage up, he'll surprise them.

Across from you are two young sisters traveling to visit their older brother in San Talpa. You hope they won't be hurt if the Burrows Gang tries to rob this stagecoach again.

Turn to page 82.

The next day you're up and riding by the first light. Before you know it, you've reached the next station.

Soon you master your route and have no problem riding seventy-five miles a day. Matt was worried about you at first, but now you have his blessing. Every time you pass through San Talpa, you stop and see him.

Other riders tell you about close calls they've had with Indians and robbers, but so far you've had no problems. Sometimes you secretly wish that something exciting would happen to you.

Go on to the next page.

One day you get your wish.
When you slow down your horse to get around a
sharp bend, two men jump out from behind some
rocks. They have bandannas over the bottom halves
of their faces and have pistols aimed at you.
They are after your valuable load of mail!

Turn to page 46.

"Hand over those mail pouches," one of the robbers demands.

Three ideas flash through your mind. The safe thing to do is to give them what they want. The riskiest choice is to try to push through and outrun them. Or maybe you can bluff your way out of this mess.

If you decide to try to push through, using your advantage in speed, turn to page 85.

If you decide to try to bluff, turn to page 71.

If you decide it's best to just hand over the pouches, turn to page 92.

"There's plenty of time for rest later," you tell your trusty steed.

Sometime later you notice a plume of smoke on the horizon.

You spur your horse on toward the smoke. Someone must be in trouble!

As you close the distance the smoke seems to fill the sky. You hear strange cries from up ahead.

Turn to page 98.

48

You report on time the next morning. A fast pony is waiting for you, already loaded with pouches of mail.

Mr. Tucker steps out of the office, hands you a pistol, and says, "I'm glad you didn't change your mind. A light and strong rider like yourself is best for this job, so I'm happy to have you working for me. Good luck."

Turn to page 73.

You grope down the dark tunnel, hoping to find a hiding place. You are no match for a desperate gang of robbers, you tell yourself.

Now you can feel the breeze on your face, and up ahead you see a beam of daylight from a gaping hole in the roof. It appears to be a crude ventilation shaft.

You realize that the top is out of your reach, so you head down the shaft to see if you can find anything that can help you escape. The robbers must have entered the mine by now. Luckily you find an ore cart within twenty yards of the ventilation shaft. After positioning the cart under the hole, you turn the cart over onto its top. Now you can stand on the flat bottom. From there the top of the shaft is within jumping distance.

You spring off the cart, and your fingers grip the edge of the shaft. Muscles straining, you haul yourself up out of the mine.

Turn to page 113.

You join the cowboys and spend the day touring the ranch and helping them with their chores. They invite you to spend the night, and you accept. After dark they entertain you with lasso tricks and folk songs.

Turn to page 77.

52

Within minutes you are cooling off in a mountain stream. The sun's rays still beat down. Your horse neighs quietly as he shuffles his head along the ground, looking for grass.

As you languish in the water you notice your horse's ears prick up. You glance around rapidly, but you don't see anything. Slowly you start to wade toward your clothes on the riverbank. A scraping sound alerts you. You spring to your feet just as a man darts out from behind a tree and grabs your gun belt. You settle back uneasily in the water. The man has your gun!

You watch as he uncaps your canteen and takes a long drink. He looks very dirty. His face is unshaven, and his hair is stringy with dried sweat. His whole body sags with exhaustion. You notice he is wearing gray flannel, just like criminals wear in prison! He has obviously been walking for hours.

"Howdy," he says through crooked teeth.

Turn to page 60.

The robbers grab the strongbox from the driver's hands and rummage through its contents.

"Ah, here it is," one bandit with a grubby beard and beady eyes says. He pulls stacks of bills from the box. "C'mon let's go," he says triumphantly.

The crooks turn to leave. Do you let them go or do you try to fight them? The odds look bad if you try to fight. Besides, Matt may have decided to wait for some reason.

On the other hand, you can't stand to let them get away with a robbery in your territory.

If you let them go, turn to page 88.

If you attack, turn to page 8.

54

Soon you are trotting into the sleepy town of Alkali City. You scan the street, looking for your horse. Sure enough, you spot it tied to the hitching post at the only saloon.

"Do you want to get the thief?" Jed asks, offering you his pistol. "Or should I?"

You realize that Jed is offering you a chance to regain your honor by capturing Coltrain yourself.

If you decide to go in after Coltrain, turn to page 14.

If you want Jed to go, turn to page 86.

You have no choice but to open fire with your rifle. The range is about one hundred yards. You take careful aim at the lead outlaw and squeeze the trigger. He's hit and falls off his horse. Quickly you fire off five more warning shots. The shots are too close for comfort for the gang. They grab their wounded member and speed off.

Turn to page 59.

You ride hard for three hours. Every so often the man stops to check the ground for the trail.

"Alkali City," he says finally.

"What do you mean?" you demand. "Who are you anyway? Who's the guy who stole my horse?" You are fed up. The man knows a lot more than he's telling.

"We'll find him in Alkali City," he says mysteriously as he hands you a folded piece of paper.

You unfold the paper. It's a wanted poster—and the picture on the poster is an exact likeness of the man who took your horse!

Excitedly you read the words on the picture:

WANTED
DEAD OR ALIVE
MORGAN COLTRAIN
WANTED FOR THEFT AND
BREAKING JAIL.
EXTREMELY DANGEROUS.
$500
REWARD!

Turn to page 68.

You continue as a Pony Express rider for the rest of the summer. When it's time for you to return to your home in the East, Uncle Matt and Mr. Tucker walk you to the stage.

"You are an excellent rider," Mr. Tucker says as he wrings your hand.

"I'm real proud of you," Matt says as you shake his hand before boarding.

The Pony Express is in existence only another year because of the invention of the telegraph. The telegraph's faster and more reliable means of communication puts the brave riders out of work. Someday you can tell your children—and their children—what it was like to be one of the few people who ever rode for the Pony Express.

The End

When you return to town, your uncle is already back at the jailhouse. You quickly fill him in on what happened.

"Good work," Matt says, clapping you on the back. "The nine o'clock stage was carrying a huge payroll. Thanks to you, it wasn't stolen."

You start to smile, but suddenly you realize that your job isn't finished yet.

"One gang member is wounded, but what's to stop the Burrows Gang from trying to rob the stage tomorrow?"

"Good point, Deputy," Matt replies. "We've got to track them down. We can look for their hideout this afternoon. Or we can let them come to us. You can ride as an extra passenger on the stage tomorrow, and I'll trail it. If the gang strikes at the stage again, we'll be able to trap them. Which plan would you like to follow?"

If you say, "Let's look for the gang today,"
turn to page 15.

If you say, "I'd like to try to trap them,"
turn to page 42.

60

The man continues. "I thought I'd plumb dry out, walkin' in the sun like thet after my horse went and died on me. Glad I made it to these mountains. O' course, I could of drunk from the stream, stead o' your canteen, but the stream water is probably less clean, seein' how yore sittin' in it!"

You can only stare at him and wonder how you'll get out of this mess. You watch as he starts pulling off his boots and socks. Then he puts his swollen feet in the water.

"Ahhh . . ." he sighs. "Thet feels great, yes sir!"

Turn to page 69.

Early the next morning you and Matt ride to Wheelerville to meet the stage. You explain to the driver that you want to ride on the stage as extra protection while Matt trails it. The driver agrees, and soon you are in the rattling, shaking stagecoach, fingering your pistol's handle nervously.

It surprises you, but the stage makes the run uninterrupted. Maybe you shook up the gang yesterday more than you thought.

In any case the Burrows Gang has moved on, because within a week they are spotted in the next state.

Turn to page 26.

You follow a roundabout course to skirt the Indian camp on the left, and it works. The journey to Fort Carson goes quickly, and you are ushered in to see the commander of the fort. He is aware of the new hostilities but doesn't know the location of their main forces until you tell him.

Within twenty minutes the full garrison of the fort heads out for battle. As for you, your western adventure is over. With the Indians on the warpath Uncle Matt decides to send you back East.

The End

You ride for an hour through the blazing western sun. As you wipe your forehead you scan the prairie. Tumbleweed blows lazily back and forth amid the cacti. The mountains are to your left. The direct route to Fort Carson is straight ahead. A few miles to your right you spot an adobe trading post that serves all the outlying cowboys and ranchers. Two horses are tied in front of the trading post. You can see a stack of colorful Indian blankets piled by the door.

Would you like to cool off? You could escape the sun by swimming in the mountain streams or by checking out the trading post. Of course, if you press on, you'll reach Fort Carson sooner.

If you go to the trading post, turn to page 83.

If you go to the mountains, turn to page 52.

If you continue traveling to Fort Carson, turn to page 47.

The summer finally comes to an end. It's time to begin the long trip home. You'll return to your family back East for the new school term.

Matt rides with you to the stage. It's time to say good-bye.

"I really enjoyed staying with you, Uncle Matt. Thanks for having me," you say, trying to hide your sadness.

"You did a real fine job as deputy. You kept law and order and protected the people in this territory. I'm real proud of you," Matt says warmly.

Turn to page 94.

After Mr. Parker rides back to his ranch house, you ask a couple of his men if they know anything about the theft of the prize longhorns. They stare at you sullenly and say they know nothing. You decide to resume your check of the outlying ranches.

When you are almost off Mr. Parker's property, a rider gallops up.

"I couldn't speak up before, but I think I know something about the rustling. Late last night the foreman rode off with about six men. I didn't think anything of it then, but now I'm convinced that they were up to no good."

"We've got to search this ranch!" you exclaim.

"I don't think so," says a gravelly voice behind you.

"The foreman!" shouts your informant.

The foreman has a Colt aimed at both of you. He gestures back toward the ranch house with his pistol.

"Move it!" he says menacingly.

Turn to page 28.

Now you know the identity of the man you're riding behind. He's a bounty hunter! You've heard about these men who hunt down criminals for a reward. They tend to be loners.

"So you've been hunting Coltrain all along— for the bounty," you state. "What's your name?"

"Jed," he answers.

You ride on in silence.

Turn to page 54.

After a fifteen-minute rest he puts on his footwear, stands up, and walks over to your horse.

"So long," he calls as he mounts your horse.

"Hey!" you shout.

He lays your pistol across his lap and says, "Don't worry. I'm jest borrowin' it. Yes sir, jest borrowin' it. Giddap!"

There's nothing you can do as he rides off, his laughter echoing among the bleak mountains.

You get dressed and take a long drink from the stream. Then you begin the long walk back to the jailhouse.

If you head straight home, turn to page 76.

If you walk to the trading post, hoping to get a ride, turn to page 32.

You decide to search the ranch for the cattle. After looking all afternoon, you come upon a small corral with about twenty steers inside. As you reach for the gate a shot rings out. The bullet throws up a shower of wood as it plows into the gatepost. You dive for cover behind a nearby tree. A few seconds later you cautiously peer out, looking for your attacker.

One of Mr. Parker's ranch hands stands about twenty yards away. He's pointing a smoking rifle right at you.

"That was your only warning shot. Come out from behind the tree right now," the man says.

Turn to page 103.

"I'm surprised that you dare to be out in these parts with all the hostile Indians around," you say, bluffing.

"Indians!" the robbers exclaim. They look at each other and then glance around to make sure no Indians are sneaking up on them.

This is your chance, you think. As soon as they take their eyes off you you spur your horse on, right past the crooks.

In order to be a smaller target you crouch down and hug your horse's neck. It works because both robbers empty their pistols at you, but all the bullets miss.

You've escaped! You can finish your route and report the attempted stickup, but on the other hand, you tell yourself, these robbers should be brought to justice. Maybe you should sneak up on them and try to capture them.

If you decide to finish your Pony Express route, turn to page 58.

If you decide to try to find and capture the robbers, turn to page 110.

You wave to him as you nervously head out on your first Pony Express run.

You keep a sharp eye out for bandits and Indians, and you make it safely to the next station before nightfall.

Inside the station—a small one-room cabin—you meet the stationmaster, Frank Dixon. He makes you a hot meal and gives you directions for tomorrow's trip. Tired and sore, you trudge off to bed.

Turn to page 43.

You are at the edge of Indian Gulch when you hear the shots up ahead. You cross the gulch rapidly and guide your horse back onto the trail. The nine o'clock stage is moving at full speed toward you, pursued by four bandits on horseback! It must be the Burrows Gang! They are wearing their trademark—navy bandannas—and have smoking pistols drawn.

Turn to page 55.

Henry doesn't offer to let you stay at his ranch, so that night you and Mr. Miller's ranch hands bed down at the edge of his property. As you lie under the starry sky you think about your conversation with the rancher. Henry sure acted suspicious. Maybe you should ignore his warning and investigate his pasture.

*If you search south tomorrow,
turn to page 100.*

*If you decide to search the North Pasture,
turn to page 18.*

It takes the rest of the day and most of the night to walk back to San Talpa.

As soon as you walk into the jail Matt showers you with questions.

"Where have you been? I was worried sick. What would your parents have done to me if you never came back? What happened?"

Glumly you explain.

You never see your horse or the thief again. The rest of your vacation you are not allowed to go more than a mile from town by yourself. Matt does take you to visit Fort Carson, though.

The End

You're sitting near the campfire when one of the men approaches. "Do you know me?" he asks.

"No, I don't," you reply.

"You don't know me? I'm the meanest, orneriest, toughest cowpoke this side of the Rio Grande! I eat Apaches for breakfast! Why, one day I killed a herd of buffalo with my bare hands because it was quicker than waiting for them to pass! I'm so strong, I can drive nails into steel with my little finger! And you never heard of me?"

By this time the men—Matt included—are roaring with laughter at the amazed look on your face. Your uncle explains that cowboys sometimes enjoy fooling inexperienced "pardners" like yourself with tall tales.

You bed down on the cool ground near the ranch house and fall asleep gazing at the stars.

Turn to page 11.

You know that one of the gang members was wounded in the attempted stage robbery. That would explain the moaning. You have to make sure, so you continue to sneak down the left tunnel.

Rounding a bend, you see light spilling from around another bend up ahead. You hear another moan. You gather your courage and inch forward. Peeking around the corner, you discover the gang's hideout. You see bedrolls spread out and a horse tied to a beam. Spilling from a carelessly tossed bag are bank notes with the distinctive logo of the National Bank of Santa Fe. The wounded crook lies in the middle of the passage with his teeth clenched and his eyes closed. You can see that he's in a lot of pain.

You creep back toward the mine's entrance. You'd better find Matt and tell him about the gang's hideout. But when you reach the main tunnel, you hear voices outside the entrance.

Go on to the next page.

"I say we hide out here for another couple o' days and then hightail it outta here," says one voice.

"How in blazes do you 'spect to make any money hidin' out?" another adds.

"Blast it! Stop arguing! We need to stick together," a different gang member shouts.

While they are arguing you slip into the right-hand shaft. . . .

Turn to page 49.

You judge that this is the time to stick to the best percentages. You meet the stage six miles from San Talpa. A team of six foaming horses pulls the bright red stage. Two men ride on top. One is the driver, and the other, riding shotgun, is a guard.

The driver slows down as the man riding shotgun eyes you warily.

"What is it, Deputy?" the driver asks.

"The Burrows Gang is in the area. I think they may try to rob the stagecoach," you respond.

"We're carrying a valuable payroll. They'd love to get their hands on that. We'll take the road that runs through the mountains," states the driver.

"Fine. I'll escort you," you reply.

The road through the mountains runs parallel to the stage's regular trail; sometimes the two routes are within sight of each other. At one of these points, about two miles from San Talpa, you notice the Burrows Gang down below. They are hiding at the base of the mountain, planning to ambush the stage.

The crooks see you too. They leap on their horses and rapidly climb the mountain after you.

Turn to page 29.

You haven't gotten far from Wheelerville when the Burrows Gang makes its move. Before you know it, you are surrounded by three men. So far everything is going according to plan. Any second now Matt will catch them unawares.

"Hand over that strongbox!" a rough-looking robber demands. "And be quick about it!"

"Hold on, I'm working on it," says the driver.

What's going on? you wonder as the driver slowly reaches under his seat for the steel cashbox. He's trying to stall. Where's Matt? He should have been here by now!

Turn to page 53.

As you approach the one-story trading post you see two men sitting outside playing checkers. They are under the shade of the only tree within five miles.

"Howdy," they say.

"Howdy," you answer as you enter the post.

Inside you find a wide variety of items from flour to rifles.

You spend more time at the trading post, looking at saddles, than you had originally planned. You have decided to buy some licorice and hit the trail again when you hear some yelling outside.

Turn to page 90.

84

You decide to stick around, gambling that you'll learn something useful. You climb a small hill, hide your horse, and lie flat to avoid detection. From your vantage point you see dozens of riders come and go.

You don't see the Indian behind you, though— the one that smashes the flat of his tomahawk against your temple.

Turn to page 16.

Slowly you reach back toward the mail pouches as if you were going to hand them over. Then you dig your spurs into your horse, and he bolts past the startled thieves.

You bend over and hug your horse's neck as bullets whiz past you. Only when the bandits are completely out of sight do you notice blood on your pant leg. The wound is not very serious, but you will be laid up for a few days. You can return to work as soon as it heals.

Turn to page 58.

"It's your bounty," you say.

"All right," Jed says with a grin.

He strolls boldly into the saloon, with his gun drawn. You peer inside anxiously. About twenty people are in the saloon, drinking and playing cards. You don't spot Coltrain, but the bounty hunter is walking purposefully toward the bar. Then he stops behind a man at the bar. He taps the man on the shoulder, and the man whirls around. It's Coltrain! He's shed his gray flannels for jeans and a shirt.

"Coltrain, you're coming in dead or alive," the bounty hunter says in a measured voice.

Turn to page 3.

Patience is called for, you decide as the robbers ride off with the strongbox. The best strategy now is to return to San Talpa and wait to hear from your uncle.

You are in the sheriff's office when Matt strides in.

"Get ready to ride," he says. "I trailed the gang to their hideout in the mountains. Now we can arrest the entire gang and recover all the loot from their earlier crimes."

You ask your uncle what made him decide not to go with the original plan.

Matt answers, "When I noticed that the wounded gang member was missing, I knew it would be better to trail them. I had no way to let you know about the change in plan, but you picked it up anyway. Good job!"

Turn to page 107.

You reach the top of the mountain but uncover no traces of the Burrows Gang. When it's time to meet Matt, you quickly ride back to your meeting place. Perhaps he's found something.

Matt arrives at the spot ten minutes after you do. He's found no trace of the gang either, so you decide to head back and go with your other plan to catch the Burrows Gang when they attempt to rob the stagecoach!

Turn to page 62.

Curious, you move to the doorway along with the owner of the trading post. Outside about a dozen cowboys on horses are surrounding a man on foot. One of the cowboys is holding one end of a rope with the other end looped around their prisoner's neck. The prisoner looks exhausted—as if he's been forced to walk for miles without rest or water. The man's hands are bound together.

Turn to page 30.

"All right. I'll do whatever you want," you answer. The bandits take the pouches of mail and your pistol. Then they ride off. You head back to town and report the robbery.

The mail is never recovered, but Mr. Tucker says you did the right thing.

Turn to page 58.

Soon after nightfall you cut through the remaining strands of your bonds and pad away into the hills. You hide out there for two days until you are found by a troop of the U.S. Cavalry.

When you get back to San Talpa, you learn that your uncle Matt was killed fighting the Indians.

Within an hour you are on the stage, traveling east. Your western vacation is over.

The End

When you shake your uncle's hand, he presses something cold and shiny into your palm. It's a sheriff's badge!

"The people of San Talpa decided to make you an honorary sheriff," Matt explains.

You are smiling when you board the stage for the long journey home.

You spend the time gazing at the shiny badge and dreaming about spending next summer in San Talpa.

The End

Rage contorts your features as you thunder down the hill, like an avenging angel, toward the nearest Indian. You scarcely notice the first Indian going down as you automatically move on to the next one. You do notice a tremendous pain when an arrow pierces your left leg.

Another Indian falls. Then you take another arrow, this one in your left side.

You don't remember riding to Fort Carson and warning the commander about the Indian uprising, but the Fort Carson corpsman, the doctor, assures you that you did. He also tells you your action saved dozens of people in the territory. You're a hero.

The End

As you tour Henry's land the group of men working on mending the pasture fence watch you and Henry anxiously. You're not surprised when Henry turns you away from a herd of cattle at the far end of the pasture. You're determined to get a look at that herd as soon as you get the chance.

"Well, I'm satisfied," you comment. "Let's head back."

Henry seems surprised but quickly agrees.

"Why don't we race back?" you suggest. "I'll bet my horse can beat yours by a hundred yards."

"I'll have you know my horse is a purebred stallion," Henry says irately. "You're on!"

Turn to page 39.

A few days later there is a meeting between the leaders of both sides. As in all negotiations, the white settlers give up certain things and so do the Indians. In the end everyone is satisfied, and your territory is now one of the most peaceful in the West.

The End

As you come to the top of a crest a chaotic scene unfolds below. A farmhouse and barn are blazing.

Three miles away you see about forty Indian warriors riding away, presumably toward the next farmhouse.

Four Indians remain near the burning house, surveying the carnage. It is obvious that the family did not escape.

You can attack the four Indians, gain some revenge, and then warn the neighboring families.

Or you can ride right away to Fort Carson and alert the garrison.

If you attack the Indians, turn to page 95.

If you ride to Fort Carson, turn to page 25.

The next day you search to the south but can find no trace of the stolen steers. You report your failure to Matt. He hasn't had any luck either.

Matt says, "We'll never find those longhorns now. Tomorrow is the day the ranchers drive their cattle east to market. By now the cattle have been rebranded and mixed in with a crooked rancher's herd."

You realize that sometimes robbers aren't brought to justice. It's a hard lesson—but one that any deputy in the West must learn.

The End

You turn your back as the mob leads the prisoner away. You know exactly what his fate is.

You've lost your enthusiasm for visiting Fort Carson, so you turn your horse around and head back to San Talpa. As you ride you realize that by not standing up to the mob, you are just as much to blame as its members. You'll never forget the look of horror on the prisoner's face.

The End

There's nothing else you can do but surrender. The man takes you back to Mr. Parker's ranch house, where you are tied up and thrown into a small dark room.

You don't know how long you'll have to wait before Matt realizes you're missing. But all you can do is hope that your uncle is as good at tracking people as he is at tracking cattle.

The End

104

You try to skirt the Indian camp on the right, but you run into two dozen warriors on horseback. There is no escape. You try to surrender, but they aren't interested in taking prisoners. . . .

The End

You choose to dash for a horse and try to use the element of surprise to flee. A lookout spots you before you have finished untying a horse, but you are able to mount up and ride for your life.

The lookout gives the alarm, and soon scores of Indians are pursuing you. You must not have picked the right mount, because soon they are within rifle range. Within seconds your horse is hit and falls. Your leg is crushed under your horse's weight.

You try to hobble away on your one good leg, but you don't get very far.

The End

You help Matt organize a posse, and then you all head for the gang's mountain hideout. You find the overconfident crooks lazily counting their loot, with no guards posted. Their mouths hang open in disbelief as you put them in irons.

Within the hour the criminals are behind bars in your small jail. With your help the sheriff of tiny San Talpa captured the notorious Burrows Gang, scourge of the West.

The End

After you finish eating, Matt gives you a tour of his town. The main businesses are Caroline's café, the general store, the Silver Dollar Hotel, the smithy, and the Bucking Bronco Saloon. Just off Main Street is the Pony Express office. Matt explains that the Pony Express is a new mail-delivery system that uses daring riders for speedy service. In the office window you see a RIDER WANTED sign.

Later that night you tell Matt that you're thinking about becoming a Pony Express rider.

Your uncle looks startled. "Well," he says, "let me train you as a deputy instead. If you're good enough after two weeks, you can be my deputy for the rest of the summer."

While you'd really like to become deputy, Matt may eventually decide not to let you fill the position—no matter how hard you train. Perhaps you should join the Pony Express instead.

*If you decide to train for deputy,
turn to page 13.*

*If you go to the Pony Express office tomorrow,
turn to page 23.*

Mr. Tucker clears his throat and continues. "The Pony Express delivers mail from Saint Joseph, Missouri, to Sacramento, California. We've been in business almost three months, and we're here to stay. Much of the territory between our stations is unsettled and very hazardous.

"You'll carry your load of mail from station to station and over one hundred-and-fifty miles a day. The entire trip must be completed in eight days. Do you still want the job?"

When you nod, Mr. Tucker continues. "A pistol is the only source of protection you'll carry. You will fight only as a last resort—your best weapon is speed."

He spends another hour giving you miscellaneous details and makes you repeat them until you learn them. Finally he says, "I'll see you at five o'clock tomorrow morning!"

Turn to page 48.

110

You circle back around, hoping to catch the robbers from behind. You succeed in surprising the crooks only a few miles from where you left them. You've got your pistol trained on them, so they put up no resistance.

After you have turned the robbers over to the law, Mr. Tucker praises you for service beyond the call of duty. Inside the envelope that holds your monthly pay you are pleasantly surprised by a nice bonus.

The End

You retrieve your horse and gallop off to find Matt. Within twenty minutes you've found him and explained the situation. You both return to San Talpa and organize a posse. Then you go back to arrest the gang. The robbers are guarding the entrance, but you surprise them from the rear by entering via the ventilation shaft. The Burrows Gang is finished—and you're a hero!

The rest of your vacation is peaceful. You spend your free time swimming in the cool mountain streams, writing long letters to your family back East, and drinking sarsaparilla in the Bucking Bronco Saloon.

The End

ABOUT THE AUTHOR

MARC NEWMAN, winner of the Choose Your Own Adventure writing contest, wrote *Longhorn Territory* at the age of seventeen, when he was attending high school in Otsego, Michigan. He attended Western Michigan University in place of his senior year, and was a National Merit Finalist in the spring of 1987. Marc has just started college, and eventually hopes to become a writer or a history professor. He enjoys playing basketball, tennis, and all games of strategy, and he collects and sells rare and collectible comic books.

ABOUT THE ILLUSTRATOR

FRANK BOLLE studied at Pratt Institute. He has worked as an illustrator for many national magazines and now creates and draws cartoons for magazines as well. He has also worked in advertising and children's educational materials and has drawn and collaborated on several newspaper comic strips, including *Annie*. A native of Brooklyn Heights, New York, Mr. Bolle now works and lives in Westport, Connecticut.

CHOOSE YOUR OWN ADVENTURE

Prices and availability subject to change without notice.

Shop at home
for quality children's books
and save money, too.

Now you can order books for the whole family from Bantam's latest catalog of hundreds of titles including many fine children's books. *And* this special offer gives you an opportunity to purchase a Bantam book for only 50¢. Here's how:

By ordering any five books at the regular price per order, you can also choose any other single book listed (up to a $5.95 value) for just 50¢. Some restrictions do apply, so for further details send for Bantam's catalog of titles today.

VARSITY COACH

The all-new, action-packed Sports Series that will keep you cheering, page after page!

☐ 26033 **FOURTH & GOAL #1**
Tommy Hallowell $2.50

☐ 26209 **TAKEDOWN #2**
Lance Franklin $2.50

☐ 26330 **OUT OF BOUNDS #3**
Tommy Hallowell $2.50

☐ 26526 **DOUBLE PLAY #4**
Lance Franklin $2.50

Look for them at your local bookstore, or use this handy coupon for ordering:

Bantam Books, Inc., Dept. CO, 414 East Golf Road, Des Plaines, Ill. 60016

Please send me _____ copies of the books I have checked. I am enclosing $_____. (Please add $1.50 to cover postage and handling.) Send check or money order—no cash or C.O.D.s please.

Mr/Ms _____

Address _____

City/State _____ Zip _____

CO—10/87

Please allow four to six weeks for delivery. This offer expires 4/88. Prices and availability subject to change without notice.